by Matthew K. Manning

illustrated by Joey Ellis

# RETURN TO PEGASIA

raintree
a Capstone company — publishers for children

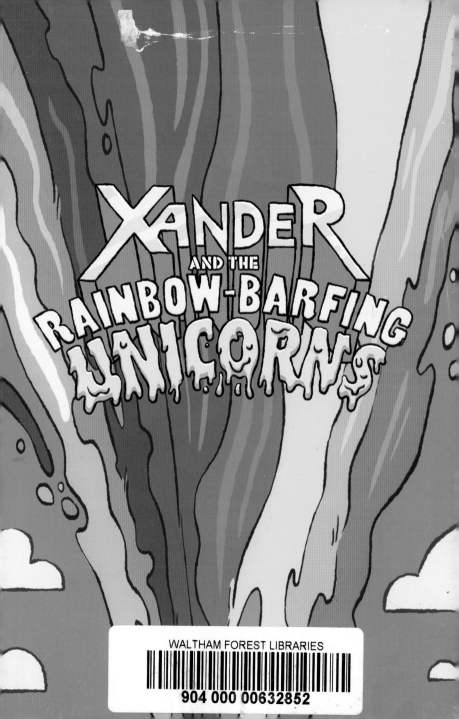

# XANDER
### AND THE
# RAINBOW-BARFING
# UNICORNS

R[...]                                                    [...]mited,
a[...]                                                    [...]ng its
re[...]                                                   [...]DY –
R[...]

w[...]
m[...]

Te[...]
The moral rights of the proprietor have been asserted.

Designed by Bob Lentz
Original illustrations © Capstone Global Library Limited 2019
Production by Kris Wilfahrt
Originated by Capstone Global Library Ltd
Printed and bound in India

ISBN 978 1 4747 5180 3
22 21 20 19 18
10 9 8 7 6 5 4 3 2 1

British Library Cataloguing in Publication Data
A full catalogue record for this book is available from the British Library.

# LEGEND SAYS . . .

The Rainbow-Barfing Unicorns
come from a faraway, magical
world called Pegasia. Not so
long ago, these stinky, zombie-
like, vomiting creatures were
banished to Earth for being, well
. . . stinky, zombie-like, vomiting
creatures. However, Earth presents
them with a new danger: humans.

So, just who are the Rainbow-Barfing
Unicorns . . . ?

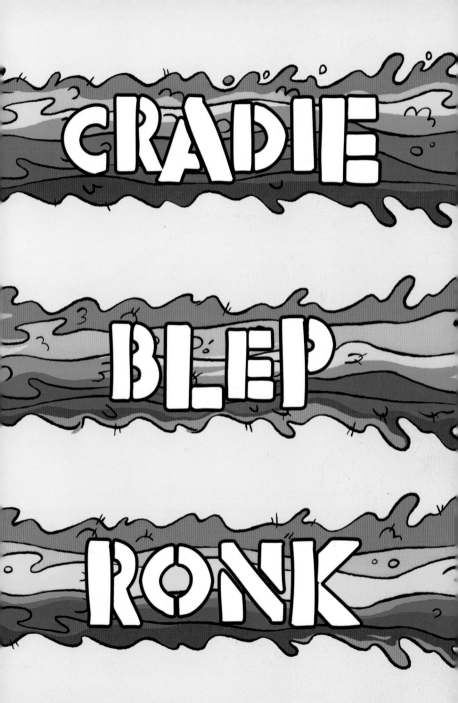

# CHAPTER ONE

Gregory's bag was heavy. He knew it was
going to be harder to carry than the last
time. Back then, the bag had been filled with
candyfloss and a few handfuls of jelly beans. But
as he ran through the Candy Cornfield, he was
surprised at exactly how much he was straining.
Ears of candy corn weigh a lot more than one
would expect.

Just a few hours ago, Gregory had been
behind his counter at Whittle's Sweet Shop,

dealing with one of his worst repeat "customers".
This particular little boy had been wandering
around the shop for over an hour. He had yet
to buy anything on any of his many visits to
Gregory's shop.

The boy seemed to prefer to simply look at the
jars of gum balls and wander down the aisle of
chocolate bars. He had even stared at the counter
for a good fifteen minutes as his eyes darted from
one sweet to the next.

"Can I help you?" Gregory had finally asked
when the clock on the wall struck six.

The boy popped his head around a display of
various hot chocolate mixes. "Me?" he asked.

"You're the only one in here," said Gregory.

The boy walked over to the counter. He turned
his head in the direction of a brown wooden door
at the back of the shop.

"What's in there?" he asked.

"That's the storeroom," said Gregory. "It's private."

The boy's shoulders slumped. He seemed a bit disappointed. "I was hoping there was some cool surprise in there or something," he said.

Gregory smiled. He looked at the wooden door for a second or two. He appeared lost in thought. "No," he finally said. "Nothing worth talking about."

Five minutes later, the boy finally left.

Three hours after that, Gregory was running through a dark field with only a bright pink moon lighting his way. It was hard for Gregory to crouch low as he moved. He was in his forties now. Nothing was as easy as it had been when he was the age of the boy in his shop. But the last thing he wanted was to be spotted.

"Hello," said a pink unicorn standing directly in front of him. She seemed to have appeared out of nowhere.

Gregory tried to stop himself. But he was still in mid-run, so that wasn't exactly possible. He slowed down just enough to trip over the small unicorn without really hurting either of them.

Nevertheless, he landed face down in the dirt.

"Oh dear!" said the unicorn. The moon seemed to spotlight her. It was as if she was the subject of a children's play. Although it would have been a play too silly for Gregory to ever waste his time or money on.

Gregory pushed himself up and to his feet.

"Are you lost?" asked the unicorn in a sing-song voice.

"Just . . . just heading home," said Gregory. He licked his lips. The dirt tasted like crushed up chocolate cookies. Of course it did.

"How exciting!" said the unicorn.

"Um, OK," said Gregory.

"You're from Earth!" said the unicorn. It wasn't a question but a very happy statement.

"Yes?" said Gregory. Oddly enough, his reply actually did seem like a question. He continued to dust himself off.

"You dropped your liquorice!" said the unicorn.

Gregory gave her a curious look and then noticed that his wallet was lying in the ground beside his feet. He bent over to pick it up.

"It's not liquorice," said Gregory.

"I bet it's delicious," said the unicorn. "Is it dark chocolate?"

"It's not edible. It's leather," he answered.

"What's *leather*?" asked the unicorn. Her smile widened.

Gregory didn't have the heart to tell her. Instead, he said, "I really must be going."

"So you have a way to get to Earth and back again?" she asked.

"Yes," said Gregory.

"Wonderful!" said the unicorn. "I've been meaning to visit your world, but I had no way of returning here."

"Well, feel free to use my portal if you're ever in town," Gregory said with a fake smile.

Of course, he didn't tell her where that portal was located. But the pink unicorn didn't even realize that until after Gregory had said his goodbyes and walked hurriedly away.

No light was on in the back room of Whittle's Sweet Shop. The room glowed naturally on its own. In the centre of the wall swirled a bright pink and white circle.

Suddenly a foot emerged from the circle. It was followed by a head and then a shoulder.

Gregory stepped into his shop's storeroom and smiled. He dropped his heavy sack onto the floor. He'd got a good haul today. He knew he had lied to the boy earlier. After all, if a portal to a magical dimension wasn't a "cool surprise", then he didn't know what was.

He opened the storeroom's back door and stepped out onto the street. Then he locked the door behind him.

# CHAPTER TWO

Xander Stone pushed his cup against the lever on his fridge. The ice maker rumbled to life. Four perfectly square cubes fell into his empty plastic cup. Xander looked down at them and sighed.

Today was the day. He was really going to do this. He was going to go outside and tell Kelly how he felt about her.

Xander walked over to the back door and paused. He wasn't good with this sort of thing. He'd had a crush on Kelly since nursery. And here he was, seven years later, about to walk outside, hand her a glass of lemonade and tell her he'd like her to be his *girlfriend*.

He looked down at the cup again. It might help if he actually put some lemonade in there.

"Get it together, Xander," he said to himself.

Xander walked over to the kitchen worktop and the row of drinks spread out on a paper tablecloth. He picked up the jug of lemonade and began to pour it.

He could do this. He knew he could.

Xander had recently discovered a whole new bold side of himself, thanks to the stage show he put on every weekend at the Montgomery Apple Orchard and Farm. He had been nervous about speaking in front of all those people at first. Soon enough, it became clear that they weren't there to see him. He was just the ringleader. The audience was there to see the Rainbow-Barfing Unicorns.

Those three zombie unicorns had changed Xander's life. The rest of the world didn't know that the Rainbow-Barfing Unicorns came from a magical land called Pegasia. They didn't know that the unicorns could talk. They didn't know that the unicorns were zombies infected by an alien virus and had to eat rubbish unless they wanted to barf up actual rainbows every time they ate. Everyone in Xander's quiet little mountain town just assumed that they were ponies playing a part in some fake magic show.

Only Xander knew the truth.

That was all because Xander had found the Rainbow-Barfing Unicorns first. They'd fallen out of some magical portal onto the mountain behind his house. He had noticed their rainbows shooting through the sky.

As a fan of the weird and unexplained, Xander had investigated immediately. He often wondered what would have happened had the Rainbow-Barfing Unicorns used a different portal and ended up somewhere else. His life would be much less interesting, that was for sure. And today, he would almost certainly not have the courage to tell Kelly what he wanted to tell her.

"Xander!" yelled a voice from behind him. It was his mum. He recognized the voice instantly.

The shrill sound snapped Xander back to reality. He glanced at the worktop. It was overflowing with lemonade. "What are you doing?" his mum yelled.

"Oops!" Xander said.

Xander stopped pouring the lemonade and put it back down. He hurried around the worktop and grabbed some kitchen roll. He started mopping up the lemonade, but it was too late. The paper tablecloth had seen its last party.

"Watch what you're doing!" his mum said. She wasn't quite yelling any more. But her voice wasn't exactly calm, either.

"Sorry," said Xander. He watched as his mum lifted the lemonade jugs off the table, wadding up the soggy tablecloth as she went.

Soon, the table had been stripped of its teal blue cloth. Xander continued to soak up the remaining sticky mess with kitchen roll.

"Just go outside," said his mum. "Let me do this."

Xander had obviously known his mum his entire life. So he knew when it was a good idea to argue with her and when it was best to get out of her way. This was a get-out-of-the-way moment if he had ever seen one.

He used a final piece of kitchen roll to clean off the sides of his cup of lemonade. Then he walked carefully to the door. The cup was filled to the brim. The last thing he wanted to do was leave a trail of sticky lemonade drops in his wake.

"Go!" his mum said again.

So Xander did just that.

Outside, Xander peered across the garden. Kelly was standing near the tree line by herself. She was patiently waiting for him. She was alone. The timing was perfect.

Xander was surprised that Kelly had found a quiet place. The garden was packed at the moment. His mum and dad rarely had barbecues. But when they did, they invited the whole neighbourhood. There were kids and adults in every corner. One group was kicking a football. Some adults were drinking from red cups on the patio. Others were sitting on garden chairs with matching red plates on their laps.

But there Kelly was, standing by his favourite oak tree and running her fingers over its bark. Kelly was just like Xander. She noticed the little things.

Xander took a deep breath and straightened up. He brushed his dark hair with his free hand. This was it. He took one cautious step and then another. The lemonade sloshed but stayed in the cup. Xander thought he was getting the hang of carrying it now.

Then he thought of his Rainbow-Barfing Unicorn friends. They were undoubtedly sleeping the day away in their stable at the orchard in the next town. He guessed they were happy to have a weekend off for the first time since they'd arrived on Earth over a month ago. Xander knew that they would be cheering him on if they were here right now.

That's when he saw the pink unicorn smile at
him from the bushes.

"What–?" Xander began. This was too much,
even for him. He knew three unicorns, and that
was strange enough. But none of his unicorn
friends were pink!

He looked at Kelly, and then back at the pink unicorn. The animal was standing directly behind Kelly at that moment. Neither Kelly nor any of the guests had noticed the odd little creature.

"What's wrong?" Kelly asked.

Xander didn't answer. He stood still with his mouth gaping open. The pink unicorn locked eyes with him.

Just then, something spooked the small, pony-like creature. It was probably Xander's shocked expression. Or it was the way Xander dropped his cup of lemonade, spilling its entire contents on his shorts in the process. But whatever the case, the pink unicorn turned and ran into the woods, back towards the small mountain's peak.

"Xander?" Kelly asked again.

Xander stared at Kelly. Then he looked down at his lemonade-covered shorts.

Then he, too, ran into the woods.

# CHAPTER THREE

"Wait!" Xander yelled. He had been running for what seemed like forever. In truth, it had been less than five minutes. "Wait! Please!"

The pink unicorn did not wait. It just kept galloping through the woods. In fact, every time Xander called after it, the unicorn seemed inspired to go even faster.

"I'm a friend!" Xander called. "I won't hurt you."

The pink unicorn sped up yet again.

Finally, the graceful animal reached the clearing at the top of the mountain. It stopped, unsure of where to run to next.

Less than thirty seconds later, Xander shot out of the tree line. When he saw the unicorn, he stopped. He was about to speak again, but then he doubled over, resting his hands on his knees. He was huffing and puffing so much, he couldn't say a word.

Not yet anyway.

Xander raised one finger towards the unicorn. It was as if he was saying, "Hold on a second."

The pink unicorn didn't run this time. The animal seemed curious about this strange, panting human creature.

"My . . .," Xander huffed. "My name . . . is . . . Xander," he finally spat out.

The pink unicorn did not answer.

"You're . . . from . . . Pegasia," Xander said.

He straightened up and rested his hands on his hips. He was out of breath, but he was trying to appear as casual as he could. He was doing a terrible job of it.

The pink unicorn's eyes widened. But it still did not answer.

"I know you can . . . that you can talk," said Xander. "I'm friends with Cradie. And Blep and Ronk."

"Grape Sorbet?" asked the pink unicorn. Her voice was high-pitched and sounded like a children's song. It wasn't gruff or scratchy like the voices of the Rainbow-Barfing Unicorns.

Xander smiled wide. "Yes!" he said. "That was Cradie's name back on Pegasia!"

The pink unicorn smiled too. It wasn't a confident smile. But it was a smile just the same. Xander would take it.

"How did you get here?" asked Xander. He had almost completely got his breath back now. Nevertheless, he felt the need to slump to the ground. Sitting would help. Anything was better than standing at the moment.

"Through the Western Portal," said the pink unicorn, "past the Banish Desert."

"Were you kicked out of Pegasia, too?" asked Xander.

"Why, no. Not exactly," said the pink unicorn. "Can you take me to Grape Sorbet?"

"To Cradie?" said Xander. "Sure! But are you . . . are you alone?"

"Yes," said the pink unicorn. "I've never been so terribly alone in all my life."

Xander raised one of his eyebrows. Not only was this unicorn's voice more like that of an old-fashioned cartoon character, she even spoke like one.

"Follow me," said Xander. "Once we get down the mountain, I'll sneak my bike out of the garage. It's got a little trailer you can ride in. You can tell me about yourself on the way. But we need to be sneaky about it."

"Because you've wet your shorts!" said the pink unicorn. She nodded at Xander's shorts.

"It's lemonade!" Xander protested.

"Yes," said the pink unicorn. "Wet with lemonade. Just as I said."

Xander looked over at this odd little unicorn as they started off through the woods. Then she really started talking . . .

# CHAPTER FOUR

And talking . . .

*My tale began on the wonderful world of Pegasia. It is a magical place where my fellow unicorns gallop in the sunshine, and the dewdrops taste of the sweetest mint. It is my home, the place where I was raised. Yes, it is truly my everything.*

*Alas, I nevertheless had to leave it.*

*My name is Bubblegum Taffy, and my best friend was Grape Sorbet. That is, before she changed her name to Cradie. Before she was banished to this world.*

*Grape and I were like sisters. We would romp through the liquorice jungle. We would play tag near the Ice Cream Cone Volcano, hoping for the sweet surprise of its cherry jam eruption. We would hop the boiled sweet stones of the chocolate milk river. Grape Sorbet and I were inseparable.*

*The only time I can remember not playing at her side was when she was out with some of our other friends in the Brown Sugar Fields. They had decided on a game of hoofball. My mother had asked for some help in the Sugarcane Cabin, so I was too busy to play that day.*

*If you can believe it, someone had been stealing the gumdrop decorations right off the walls! Crime is a rather new thing in Pegasia, and none of us were ready for it. But none of us were ready for what happened next, either.*

*I still remember the look on Custard Cream*

*Crunch's face when he knocked on the cabin's door. My mother had been worried I wasn't eating enough sweets. So at the time, I was standing at the kitchen table, munching on a freshly prepared bowl of chocolate morsels. I remember I swallowed one the wrong way when I heard Custard Cream pounding on the door. It caused just the worst coughing fit!*

*"Bubblegum!" Custard Cream Crunch had shouted when I finally answered. "Come quickly! It's terrible!"*

*The two of us galloped over to the hospital as fast as our little hooves could carry us. After we were given our complimentary lollipops, we rushed right back to Grape Sorbet's room. She was lying on her bed like a sad, pathetic little thing. She barely had the strength to munch on the green apple candy straws that lined her room's floor. She wasn't her usual purple self at all. Her colour looked faded. It was as if she had been left out in the sun for far too long.*

*Our friend Lemon Drop had arrived before me. She looked over at Custard Cream and me. Her expression said it all. "It's not good," she whispered.*

*"I can hear you," said Grape Sorbet. She looked up at us. You can imagine my surprise when she didn't smile. What kind of unicorn doesn't smile when greeted by friends? Why, it's simply unheard of!*

*"Grape," I said. "How are you? They said you breathed in some sort of . . . alien virus?"*

*"Yep," she said. As hard as it is to believe, Grape seemed almost bored. I couldn't understand what was happening. As I've said, I've lived my entire life in Pegasia. No one was ever bored there. Why would they be? It's a magical place of dreams and wonder!*

*But I'm getting off the topic . . .*

*Grape finished chewing a strand of candy straw. Then her eyes seemed to bulge a bit. She looked at Lemon Drop and then at me. Her cheeks puffed.*

*It was all so horrible! I feel faint just recounting the experience!*

*"Cradie!" she exclaimed. And as sure as I'm standing here, it happened. She . . . I don't know how to say this in polite company . . . but she barfed a rainbow.*

*It was certainly beautiful, I will say that. It was a perfect beam of multi-coloured light. It was as clear and as vibrant as any rainbow visible on Pegasia after a nice shower of refreshing limeade.*

*But it came out of her mouth, and that somehow made this beautiful thing disgusting. It was shocking. I had never seen anything that could be described as*

41

"gross" before. Things on Pegasia don't come in that particular shade.

Grape Sorbet and I locked eyes. She must have seen the disgust in my expression. I'm still so ashamed of that moment. Then she just looked away. It was as if she had not barfed a rainbow at all.

Anywho, what happened next was even worse.

Lemon Drop walked over closer to Grape. "Are you OK, sweetie?" she asked. Grape didn't answer. All she did was sniff Lemon Drop's front hoof.

"You smell," Grape began. "You smell delicious."

"Why, thank you!" said Lemon Drop. It was easy to see that she was pleased by the compliment.

In the next second, she would be quite the opposite. Because that's when Grape Sorbet tried to eat Lemon Drop's hoof!

Lemon got away, of course. It took several doctors and nurses to hold Grape back, but everyone was safe.

*It was like something had taken hold of poor Grape Sorbet. That alien gas or virus or whatever she had breathed in – it had changed my best friend.*

*And it had changed her for the worse.*

*Before I could visit Grape again, the council made their decision. Grape Sorbet and her other infected friends were to be banished from Pegasia . . . forever.*

*The really sad part was, I never got to say goodbye. I had the chance, but I didn't take it. I was too scared. I was too sad. These weren't emotions I had ever known before. So I just stayed in my room and ate my chocolate morsels. And I cried for my friend. I cried the sweetest tears you could ever see.*

*That was a month ago.*

*I've had time since then to think about what I did. I had time to miss Grape – or Cradie, as she calls herself now. And simply put, I couldn't take feeling sad any longer. So I sneaked out of my room, out of my stable and all the way across the Banish Desert to the Western Portal.*

*I looked at that magic swirling doorway, and I leaped right through.*

*The next thing I knew, I was standing on a strange mountain. (And to make matters worse, there wasn't even a cherry on its top.) This is a weird place, this Earth. But I intend on finding Cradie. I will say goodbye to my friend if it's the last thing I do. I will see Grape Sorbet again, by golly.*

*Even if she tries to eat me.*

# CHAPTER FIVE

By the time Xander and Bubblegum Taffy arrived at their destination, Xander was ready for a nap. He wasn't tired from the bike ride. No, he was thoroughly exhausted from listening to Bubblegum's story told in her sickly sweet voice.

Xander knew she meant well. But that didn't make her high-pitched tone any easier to take.

"We're here," he said, interrupting what he believed was a new poem that Bubblegum was currently working on.

"Oh," said Bubblegum Taffy. "It's so . . . it's so magical!"

Xander looked at the gates to the Henderson Landfill in front of them. Then he glanced back at Bubblegum Taffy's overly excited face.

"You think the dump is magical?" he said.

"I don't even know what a dump is!" Bubblegum squealed.

"Oh boy," Xander said. He reached into his pocket and pulled out a tiny, clear plastic case. He popped it open and put in a pair of nose plugs.

"Sorry," he said. "I only have the one pair."

"That's quite all right!" said Bubblegum. She smiled at Xander in silence for a good thirty seconds before he finally turned away.

"*Oookay,*" he said. Then he walked through the gates of the Henderson Landfill.

Bubblegum Taffy trotted beside Xander at first. The further into the rubbish dump they got, the more she seemed to lag behind. She had never seen rubbish before. She had certainly never seen a mountain of broken toilets or piles of way too many used nappies.

By the time they reached the centre of the landfill, Bubblegum was almost hiding behind Xander's legs.

"Cradie?" Xander called. "Blep?"

"**RONK!**" came a voice from behind a pile of broken computers.

"Brace yourself," Xander said to Bubblegum Taffy. She was already hiding completely behind him. She wasn't sure how she could brace herself any further.

**"RONK!"** Ronk brayed as he quickly galloped towards them.

As the messiest of the Rainbow-Barfing Unicorns, Ronk could be a bit intimidating. From his sickly green skin to his mismatched yellow eyes, he took a bit of getting used to.

"Ah!" Bubblegum screamed.

(OK, Ronk took a lot of getting used to.)

Ronk leaped onto Xander. It was all Xander could do to keep from falling down. "Hi, Ronk," he said. "Calm down, buddy. We have a guest."

Ronk was too busy rubbing up against Xander's legs to really listen to him. It seemed like it was his personal mission to make sure Xander's shorts were as filthy as possible at all times.

"Ronk," said Xander. "I'd like you to meet Bubblegum Taffy."

"We've met," Bubblegum said. She stepped timidly out from behind Xander. "Before he was a . . . what did you call him? A Ronk?"

"Oh yeah," said Xander. "Of course you've met."

"RONK?" Ronk said. He seemed to be noticing Bubblegum for the first time.

"Ronk," said Xander. "I'd like you to re-meet Bubblegum Taffy."

"Um, hi," said Bubblegum.

Xander noticed her tremble a little. She was doing her best to disguise her fear. But it wasn't quite good enough.

"Bubblegum?" said a raspy female voice.

Xander and the others turned to see Cradie slowly trotting into view.

"Bubblegum Taffy?" she said again. It was as if Cradie had to convince herself that what she was seeing was real.

"Grape?" said Bubblegum. "I mean . . . Cradie?"

"Hey, what's all the noise about–" Blep began to say as he followed Cradie into the clearing in the middle of the dump. "Whoa!" he said. "Hey, I know you!"

Cradie wandered closer. She sniffed the air. While Bubblegum was smiling at her, Cradie's face became deathly serious.

"You shouldn't be here," Cradie said.

"I had to come," said Bubblegum to her faded purple friend. "I missed you ever so much and–"

Cradie's head twitched. It was a weird spasm. Bubblegum had never seen her do anything like that before. Well, she'd seen it once before. Cradie had moved like that in the hospital back on Pegasia.

"Cradie?" Xander said. "Are you OK?"

"Tell her to go," Cradie said to Xander. She locked eyes with him. Beside Cradie, Blep was sniffing the air like a crazy person. Or a crazy unicorn, at any rate.

"What?" Xander asked. He was confused and more than a little worried.

"She . . . she can't be here," said Cradie. She twitched again, this time with her whole body.

Next to her, Blep did the same. If it wasn't for his faded red colouring, he would have looked almost like a mirror image of Cradie.

Xander turned towards Bubblegum Taffy. "I think we should go," he said.

"I don't understand!" Bubblegum protested. She seemed hurt.

"Go!" Cradie yelled.

At that, Bubblegum's fear overtook her sadness. She began to back away from her former friend.

That's when she

noticed Ronk.

The green unicorn was staring at her. His yellow eyes were wide and wild. What was worse, he was foaming at the mouth!

"RONK!" he brayed.

And Bubblegum Taffy began to run.

# CHAPTER SIX

Xander's nose plugs fell off when he picked up Bubblegum Taffy. But it couldn't be helped. She wasn't running fast enough. She wasn't as heavy as the Rainbow-Barfing Unicorns. Part of that could be because she was a bit smaller than them. But then there was also the fact that the Rainbow-Barfing Unicorns felt as dense as a laundry bag soaked in dirty water.

Bubblegum, on the other hand, felt like she

had all the heft of a stuffed toy. Xander
assumed a diet of candyfloss would do that
to a unicorn.

Xander pushed open the back gate to the
Montgomery Apple Orchard and Farm.

*Pfft!* He took a second from watching where
he was going to look down at the unicorn in
his arms. For a brief instant, he smelled the
overwhelming odour of a stick of bubblegum.

"What was that?" he managed to blurt out.

"Sorry," said Bubblegum. She seemed
embarrassed. "I tend to toot when I'm scared."

Xander didn't respond. He was nearly out of
breath, and he wasn't sure what to say even if he
could talk.

*Pfft!*

He pretended not to hear the second
bubblegum-scented toot. Running from a hungry

zombie unicorn was already weird enough. Why complicate things?

**"RONK!"**

He could hear Ronk braying madly behind them. The Rainbow-Barfing Unicorn seemed to be gaining on them. Xander made a hard turn around the stall that sold apple doughnuts. He had no destination in mind. He had no idea where to go or what to do. This wasn't the type of thing he'd planned for.

Then he saw his only hope. There was a row of portable toilets next to the fence line. Xander gritted his teeth and picked up his speed.

**"RONK!"**

No matter how fast Xander ran, Ronk was still gaining on them.

*Pfft!* (And Bubblegum Taffy was proving to be no help at all.)

"Hold on!" Xander yelled as he approached the closest toilet. Luckily for him, the sign near the door handle read "vacant".

"RONK!"

Ronk dived through the air. His chipped and mismatched teeth nipped at Bubblegum's hooves. Another centimetre and he would have chomped onto her. But he didn't have that centimetre, and he fell to the ground instead.

Xander pulled open the door to the toilet as Ronk got to his feet. He shoved Bubblegum inside, and then threw himself inside too.

Ronk dived at them again just as Xander slammed the door shut. Xander was quicker, and the next sound he heard wasn't a "RONK!" It was the sound of a Rainbow-Barfing Unicorn thumping against a closed door.

Xander slid the lock into place. He leaned

against the door, huffing and puffing like crazy. Then he turned to look at Bubblegum Taffy.

"It smells something awful in here," she said.

*Pfft!*

"Oh," said Xander. "Well, that helped a bit."

# CHAPTER SEVEN

Twenty minutes is pretty much all anyone can stand to be locked in a hot portable loo. It's too much, really. If it hadn't been for Bubblegum's particularly gross version of a home-made air freshener, Xander doubted he could have lasted as long as he did.

But at the twenty-minute mark, he simply couldn't take the heat or the stench any longer. So he opened the heavy plastic door.

"Lock it behind me, please," he said to Bubblegum Taffy.

"Do I have to?" she asked.

"For now," Xander answered. He gave Bubblegum a concerned look. He doubted there was anything as stinky as a portable loo in Pegasia.

Xander slid out of the door without opening it fully. He immediately felt the cool breeze on his skin and sweaty hair. It made him feel even sorrier for Bubblegum Taffy. It also made him want to speed things up all the more.

"Ronk?" he said, looking from side to side at the empty field of grass in front of him.

There was no answer.

"Cradie?" Xander called. "Blep?"

There was still no answer. So Xander walked back to the Henderson Landfill's rear entrance.

He moved carefully, yet quickly. Poor Bubblegum was still trapped in her plastic stink-prison.

When he saw the rainbow shoot out from the middle of the dump, Xander increased his speed.

"Guys?" he said as he reached the clearing at the centre of the landfill.

"Over here," Cradie said from around a corner of old books and newspapers that should have been taken to a recycling plant in the first place.

Xander rushed towards her familiar voice. He wasn't expecting what he saw next . . .

Cradie, Ronk and Blep were all wearing the reins they wore during their stage show. Each had been tied to a large piece of broken old machinery that Xander guessed originally had something to do with farming.

"Not bad for having no hands," Cradie said. She smiled at Xander but didn't seem happy.

"You tied yourselves up?" Xander asked.

"Cradie did the tying," said Blep. "I just went along with it. Ronk, not so much."

"RONK," Ronk said. He sounded like he was pouting.

"It's for Bubblegum's safety," said Cradie. "I'm getting better at managing this . . . *craving*, but it's not easy. Seems worse for Ronk."

"Craving?" Xander asked. He was afraid to hear the answer.

"We wanna eat our friend," said Blep.

"You want to . . . *eat* her?" Xander said. His mouth was hanging open.

"It's the virus," said Cradie. "Combine that with the fact that she smells so much like sweets, and we can't control ourselves."

"It's part of the whole zombie thing," said Blep. "Kinda in the job description."

"Weird," said Xander. "This is all so very, very weird."

"Tell us about it," said Blep. He sat down and rolled his eyes.

"So what do we do now?" asked Xander.

"We get her out of here," said Blep.

"Back to Pegasia," said Cradie. "It's the only way to keep her safe."

"RONK," Ronk complained. His pouting had got worse.

"The only thing is," Cradie continued, "we have no idea how to get back."

"The portal was a one-way ride," added Blep.

"Oh boy," said Xander. He sat down next to Blep. "So what do we–" Xander stopped talking when he noticed that Blep's head was twitching. A tiny bit of drool was forming at the corner of the zombie unicorn's mouth.

Xander looked in the direction that Blep was staring. Bubblegum Taffy rounded the corner. "I know how to get home," she said. "I can take us all there."

"You can?" asked Xander. He looked to his friends to see what they thought of this dramatic statement. But all three of them were too busy drooling to do much else.

# CHAPTER EIGHT

"I'm starting to think it was a mistake to come here," said Bubblegum as she led Xander down Whittle Street. Bubblegum Taffy was the only unicorn not wearing reins at the moment. The three Rainbow-Barfing Unicorns were all tied to Xander's bike as he walked it down the empty street.

"You think so?" Xander said, jokingly.

"I came to apologize to Grape . . . er . . .

Cradie," said Bubblegum. "But I can't even talk to her when she's like this."

"Exactly. That's why we should have left her back at the Orchard," said Xander. He glanced over at Cradie. Her eyes were fixed on Bubblegum. She was licking her lips at the moment. (Or licking whatever passed for lips on a zombie unicorn.)

"No," said Bubblegum. "She'll snap out of it soon enough. You can tell she's trying."

Xander looked again at Cradie. The purple zombie unicorn faked a smile. It looked more like a grimace.

"If you say so," said Xander.

Despite appearances to the contrary, Cradie was all dolled up at the moment. That's what Blep called the process. Before Xander ever took the Rainbow-Barfing Unicorns out in public, he made sure they had on their stage make-up. He covered them in various shades of thick powder, blusher and foundation. The result made them look less like zombies and more like Earth ponies dressed up to look like fake unicorns.

The make-up got them plenty of stares on the street. But no one called the police or the FBI. People just smiled and went on with their day. Almost no one expects to see real magic out and about in the world.

"So where is this place?" asked Xander.

"121 Whittle Street!" Bubblegum exclaimed in her usual happy voice.

"And how exactly do you know that?"

"Because that's what the man's card said."

"The man," said Xander. "Wait, you're from Pegasia, but you've met a man? A *human* man?"

"Yes!" said Bubblegum Taffy. "And I was ever

so worried I would never see him again. But he had dropped a little rectangle with a shop's name and address typed on it. He had dropped it right next to me in the Candy Cornfields."

"A business card?" asked Xander.

"That's right! It tasted terrible!" she replied.

"You ate his business card," Xander repeated.

"But I did not enjoy it. I don't mind saying so."

"I don't understand any of this," said Xander.

"Before I ate it, I memorized this address. In case I ever had to use his portal, you see."

Xander looked at Bubblegum Taffy with an even more confused expression on his face. "You met a man from Earth who owns a portal to Pegasia?"

"You are very good at listening to stories!" Bubblegum said. Her already wide smile widened. "And just in time! We're here! 121 Whittle Street!"

The door to Whittle's Sweet Shop chimed when Xander pushed it open.

"Sorry, sir," said a voice from behind the counter. "We don't allow pets–" The man stopped speaking when he noticed the familiar pink unicorn standing by Xander's side.

"Hello again!" Bubblegum said.

"Bubblegum!" Xander exclaimed. "You can't just talk in front of–"

"But he's my very good friend!" Bubblegum interrupted.

"I . . . I am?" said the thin man behind the counter. He had dark circles under his eyes and light grey hair that seemed not to match his face.

"You are Gregory of Whittle's Sweet Shop on 121 Whittle Street, and I've missed you so, so much!" said Bubblegum Taffy.

"You're that unicorn from the field . . ."
Gregory said. His voice trailed off. He seemed
suddenly lost in his own thoughts.

"And I have need of the portal
you offered!" said Bubblegum.

"I don't . . . I . . ." Gregory
stumbled. "I mean . . . sure,"
he finally said. "Right
this way."

Without another word, Gregory walked to the back of the shop towards a wooden door. He pushed it open and then disappeared from sight.

"I told you he was wonderful!" said Bubblegum Taffy as she trotted after the shopkeeper.

"No you didn't," said Xander. But Bubblegum didn't seem to be listening.

# CHAPTER NINE

Xander stared at the portal in the storeroom. He seemed to be the only one impressed by the swirling circle of light. Apparently, this sort of thing was common in Pegasia.

"Well, off you go," said Gregory. He gestured to the portal with both hands like a ringleader announcing a circus act that he had seen hundreds of times.

"Thank you ever so much, my dear, dear friend," said Bubblegum Taffy.

"We only met that one time–" Gregory began to say, but Bubblegum had already leaped through the portal.

"And I can get back this way?" Xander said. "Back to Earth, I mean." He was feeling a little conflicted.

Ever since Xander had heard of Pegasia, he'd wanted to visit it. But now that it was a possibility, it seemed terrifying. What if they got stuck there? What if he couldn't breathe their weird air, or he managed to catch that alien zombie virus? What made things worse was that Xander seemed to be the only one concerned.

"Sure," said Gregory. Something in the bored way Gregory said that word put Xander even less at ease.

"I want to go home, Xander," said Cradie. Surprised, Xander looked down at his purple unicorn friend. She seemed completely back to normal.

"Cradie?" he said.

"We like it here," she said in a calm, totally normal voice. "But Pegasia is our home."

He thought about it for a second.

"She's right, bud," said Blep. He, too, seemed completely normal.

"RONK!" Even Ronk was normal now. Or as normal as Ronk got.

"OK," said Xander. "I'm in."

He watched Cradie, Ronk and Blep leap through the swirling light, one by one.

"You, too," said Gregory. He seemed a bit impatient all of a sudden. Xander frowned.

Xander shook out his arms as if he was about to perform some gymnastic feat. He cracked his neck and then stepped through the portal. Almost by instinct, he held his breath.

# CHAPTER TEN

When Xander finally allowed himself to breathe, he nearly gagged on the smell. It wasn't a bad odour. It was quite the opposite, actually. The air smelled like the sweet shop, only stronger. It was as if the air was thick with sweet smelling artificial air fresheners. It was overwhelming in a way.

In front of Xander was something like a pink wall. But that wasn't exactly right. The more he examined it, the more he realized that it wasn't a wall at all. Xander was standing in a cave of some sort. He was staring at the back of a waterfall. A pink waterfall.

He stuck out his hand and let the pink liquid splash against it. He cupped a bit of the stuff and brought it to his nose. He sniffed it. Then he took a sip. It was strawberry milk.

Xander took a step away from the waterfall. (Or was it a *milk*fall? He wasn't sure what to call it.) The rock underneath him was wet from the splashing liquid, and he hadn't realized that yet. Xander slipped, but caught himself with one hand on the side of the cave wall.

The orange "rock" chipped a little, revealing a green layer and a yellow layer underneath. It was as if this entire massive rock formation was made up of hard boiled sweets.

"Keep it together," he heard Cradie say to Blep

from the other side of the falls. It wasn't until that moment that Xander realized that he was alone in the boiled sweet cave.

Xander took a moment to survey his surroundings. In front of him flowed the milkfall. Behind him swirled the pink and white portal to Whittle's Sweet Shop on Earth. But it was what was to his left that interested him. A bit of sunshine peeked in from behind the falls.

Xander carefully put one foot in front of the other and followed the light. It led down a tunnel through the boiled sweet cliff, one that was pierced by holes in its ceiling. A patch of light shone in here. Another there. Xander followed the strange tunnel until it emptied out directly into the light of a brilliant, beautiful day.

He took a step into what looked like grass, but the texture was all wrong. Blep, Cradie and

Ronk were talking nearby, but Xander couldn't see them yet. The sunlight was so intense, it took his eyes a while to adjust. Somehow, the sun here smelled impossibly of lemon.

When his vision cleared, Xander walked across a patch of the green, grass-like plants. He turned a corner around the orange cliffside, where a clearing waited for him beyond.

The bright blue sky hovered above Cradie, Blep, Bubblegum Taffy and Ronk. A few pink clouds dotted the view. There weren't enough of the candyfloss-like things to cast any shadows on the clearing, however. The first thing Xander noticed was that Cradie was holding Blep's reins in her mouth. The second thing was that she was standing on the end of Ronk's lead as well.

Bubblegum Taffy stood nearby, watching her friends with wide, worried eyes.

"*Grr . . .*" Blep groaned. The noise reminded Xander of a growling tiger trapped in a zoo. It was like he was used to being angry, but still wasn't ready to accept his fate.

"Blep," Cradie said in a calm voice. Her head twitched.

"Is everybody OK?" Xander asked.

He knew everybody was certainly not OK.

"It's too much for us," said Cradie. She twitched again.

"So . . . hungry," said Blep.

Xander leaned down and plucked a strand of the strange grass. He was right.

It wasn't grass at all. It was something like green liquorice. He pulled a handful of it out of the ground. Then he threw it at Blep.

Without thinking, Blep gobbled up the strange plant. Blep then leaned his head back, pointed his mouth to the sky, and barfed an impressive rainbow.

"*Ooooooooh,*" said Bubblegum quietly to herself. "So pretty."

"Better?" asked Cradie.

"Better," said Blep.

With things under control, Xander took a second to examine Ronk. The sickly green zombie unicorn was busy gobbling up patches and patches of the liquorice grass.

"RONK!" he brayed. Ronk barfed a rainbow even more impressive than Blep's.

Bubblegum "ooohed" once more. She was louder this time.

"Stop that!" said a stern, yet almost silly voice from the shade of a nearby tree. Xander turned his head to see who was speaking.

Instead, he was quickly distracted by the tree itself. It seemed to be made entirely of chocolate. Its leaves were white. Upon further inspection, they looked as if they were moulded out of white chocolate. Xander wasn't a zombie unicorn, but even he was finding it difficult not to drool in this weird world.

Xander's mind snapped back to reality when a figure walked out of the shadows. Then three more unicorns walked into the light. There were four more behind them as well. None of the unicorns looked particularly excited to see their visitors.

"We should have known it was you," said the serious voice.

"Mayor Shortbread," said Cradie.

"That's Mayor Sprinkle Shortbread the Third to outsiders like you," said the mayor in her serious voice. Then she giggled. It sort of undermined her authority, Xander thought.

"Don't worry," Blep interrupted. "We ain't staying."

"That's what you think!" said the mayor. She giggled again. "Show them to their prison cells!"

*Pfft!*

Xander didn't have time to glance over to Bubblegum Taffy. He knew the sound came from her, so there was no real need to acknowledge it.

Besides, he was much too preoccupied watching a unicorn snap candy cane handcuffs around his wrists.

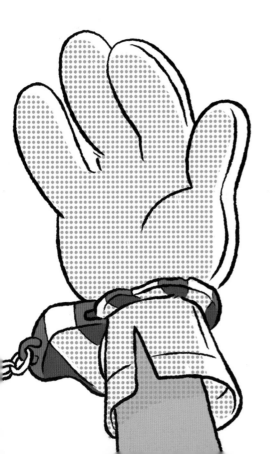

# CHAPTER ELEVEN

"**BLEP!**" Blep heaved from across the prison cell. A beautiful – yet somehow disgusting – display of rainbow light shot through the room.

The prison was a new addition to Pegasia. Cradie had certainly never seen it. As she stood in the corner, doing her best not to eat the candy straw flooring, she took in the small room. The windows and one cell wall were completely barred. The bars were made of candy canes, of course, rather than metal. They were swirling

poles of thick candy. They were certainly sturdy enough to hold in prisoners, as were the triple-enforced gingerbread walls.

Cradie glanced over at Xander. He and Bubblegum Taffy leaned against one of the walls. Ronk and Blep sat near the bars on the floor. They were staring outside into the corridor of this newly constructed police station.

Both zombie unicorns were attempting to stick their heads through the openings between the bars. Both seemed to be drooling at the sweet smelling unicorns milling about the station.

It took all the inner strength Cradie had not to join her friends. She could smell the lovely scents of the two new police officers: Chocolate Milkshake and Cinnamon Sugar.

*Pfft!* Cradie watched as Xander gave Bubblegum Taffy a look. When he realized the sound hadn't come from her, he peered out into the corridor. A strong whiff of cinnamon drifted into the prison cell.

"Was that–?"

"This place is called Pegasia for reason," said Cradie. "PeGASia," she said again, holding the middle part of the name for emphasis.

Xander thought about this for a moment. He seemed like he wanted to both laugh and cringe. Cradie imagined that would be his reaction to many things in her world.

"This place is weird," Xander finally said.

"You're not helping your case much," said the voice of Mayor Sprinkle Shortbread III. She looked serious, yet had a polite smile on her face.

No one in Pegasia enjoyed being angry or even gruff. It simply wasn't fun. And if things weren't fun, they weren't worth doing in Pegasia.

"Oh, um . . . sorry?" said Xander.

Mayor Sprinkle Shortbread III stood outside their prison cell. She had a regal air about her. Her pink mane sparkled in the bright lights of the station, as did her pink eyes and perfectly groomed golden coat. Cradie could smell her from the back of the cell. She smelled like the sweetest cake ever baked.

"Why are you keeping us here?" Cradie asked. She was suddenly angry. Her frustration had built into something like rage. "And since when did Pegasia even have a police station?"

"Since you people began stealing from us," said Mayor Shortbread.

Her serious voice was once again interrupted by her own giggle.

"Stealing from you?" protested Cradie. "You banished us from Pegasia! We haven't been back since!"

"**BLEP!**" Blep brayed from across the cell. Another rainbow shot through the room.

*Pfft!* It was as if Bubblegum felt the need to respond.

Cradie did her best to ignore the sweet bubblegum scent currently wafting through the prison cell. In reality, it only made her more frustrated, which only made her angrier.

"If anything, you stole from us!" Cradie said. "You stole our lives away when you sent us to Earth!"

"But yet here you are," said Mayor Shortbread. "Caught with your hooves in the sweet jar."

"What are you even talking about?" Cradie said. Her voice sounded raspier than usual.

"Don't pretend like you don't know," said the mayor. "We haven't located yours yet, but two-way portals are illegal in Pegasia. That's the law."

Cradie grunted. She had indeed heard this rule since she was a foal. However, this was the first time she had heard it referred to as a "law".

"And if that wasn't bad enough, we know you've been stealing from the Candy Cornfield, plucking gumdrops from our very houses, mining hot chocolate powder for your own nefarious ends. The list goes on and on!" Mayor Shortbread was doing her best to contain her own anger.

"BLEP!"

*Pfft!*

"Would you knock it off!" Cradie yelled at Blep. Then she glared at Bubblegum Taffy.

Neither unicorn responded.

"None of that was us," said Cradie to Mayor Shortbread. "If we're guilty of anything, it's of bringing Bubblegum Taffy back home. Yes, we wanted to come back, too, but we now know as well as you that we don't belong here any more."

"We'll see what the courts say," said Mayor Shortbread with a giggle.

"You have courts now too?" Cradie said. The mayor didn't answer her. She simply giggled again and trotted out of the police station without looking at Blep or any of the other Rainbow-Barfing Unicorns. Cinnamon Sugar and Chocolate Milkshake followed her to the door at the end of the corridor.

"What's up with you?" Cradie said, turning her anger towards Blep.

"If you've finished trading insults with our respected mayor, you can give me a hand," Blep said. He backed away from the bars of the prison cell.

For the first time, Cradie could see what he'd been up to. He had gnawed through an entire candy cane bar and a good portion of the one next to it. Ronk was chewing on one now, too.

"RONK!" Ronk said as he barfed a tiny rainbow.

Cradie smiled. She had never broken out of a prison before.

"Save me the butterscotch one," she said.

# CHAPTER TWELVE

It wasn't dark in the police station later that night. It should have been. The lights were turned off. It had been Chocolate Milkshake's idea.

"How else am I supposed to get some rest?" he had said. "A unicorn needs a good twelve hours of sleep to keep the grumps away!"

Cradie had cringed at the word "grumps". Had she ever been that sickly sweet?

Now, at nearly midnight, with the lights off and Cinnamon Sugar and Chocolate Milkshake snoring out in the corridor, Cradie's prison cell was still quite bright. Yes, the full moon creeping in through the window was part of it, even if the candyfloss clouds did their best to hide the brightly glowing orb. But the real reason it was so bright in their cell was from all the rainbow barfing.

**"BLEP!"**

As Blep's latest light masterpiece shot through the air, Cradie examined the prison bars. She, Ronk and Blep had done a good job with them. Bubblegum Taffy had tried to help, but she just didn't have the stomach for it.

That was probably due to all the retching and hurling from the Rainbow-Barfing Unicorns.

Cradie understood. But to be perfectly honest, she was doing her best to ignore Bubblegum Taffy. The less she thought about her friend, the less she wanted to devour her. And make no mistake about it, Cradie still really, really wanted to eat her friend right up.

Ronk jutted his head forward to chomp on another candy cane bar.

"Wait, Ronk," said Cradie. "We've finished."

Ronk backed away. Even his rather wonky mind could comprehend it. The Rainbow-Barfing Unicorns had eaten a hole right through the bars. The hole was large enough to allow each of them to pass. Even Xander could fit through if he sucked in his belly a bit.

Cradie shot a look down the corridor at the

"police officers". They were still sleeping soundly. It was time to go.

Cradie led the way, with Blep and Ronk hot on her heels. Bubblegum was next. The worried pink unicorn made sure she stayed a good distance behind her friends. She was not the least bit comfortable with the way they gazed at her. She didn't intend on becoming a delicious dessert any time soon.

Xander took up the rear of the bizarre little parade. He seemed as nervous as Bubblegum.

*Pfft!*

Well, almost as nervous.

The group tip-hoofed past the dreaming officers and out of the front door. It wasn't locked. Locks were rarely used in Pegasia. The lock on her prison cell door was the first Cradie had ever seen there.

Once her group was safely out of the station, Cradie began to pick up speed. The others followed suit. Cradie still remembered Pegasia rather well, especially the centre of town. So she was easily able to stick to its darkest corners.

She led the others past the closed post office and its edible stamps. They slunk around the Botanical Gardens and its display of chocolate roses. Cradie noticed the crushed cookie-earth overrun with delicious gummy worms. She even marched them through the quarry, effortlessly avoiding the mounds of flavoured sugars.

Within fifteen minutes, the troupe was through the golden foil-wrapped city gates. They were on their way into one of Pegasia's many thick forests.

When they finally reached the Strawberry Milkfalls, Cradie froze in her tracks. She looked back at Bubblegum Taffy. Something in her expression caused Bubblegum's heart to race.

*Pfft!*

The sweet smell of gum filled the air. Ronk licked his lips.

"What?" said Bubblegum.

"You can't come with us," said Cradie.

"So she stays," said Blep. "Big whoop."

"If she stays, she goes back to prison," said Cradie. "For a crime she didn't commit."

"And if she goes with us," said Xander. "You guys will just try to eat her all the time. So that's not an option."

"So what, we gotta play detective now?" asked Blep. "Find the true sweet thief and whatnot?"

"Somebody hasn't been paying attention," Cradie said with a smirk. When she glanced back at Blep to gauge his reaction, he was too busy eating a wild patch of chocolate-covered strawberries to answer.

"That ought to work just fine," said Cradie.

# CHAPTER THIRTEEN

Cradie had told Blep to keep eating, so that was what he was going to do. He had tried to restrain himself the entire time they were in Pegasia. But he just couldn't do it any longer. He had already munched through half of the chocolate-covered strawberry patch by the time Ronk trotted over to join him.

Blep was aware that Cradie had left. He just didn't really care too much at the moment. These strawberries weren't going to eat themselves. If only he didn't have to take a break every minute or so to—

"BLEP!" Blep brayed.

A rainbow shot from his mouth into the evening air. He wasn't sure how many rainbows he had barfed since he started this particular snack. Ten? Maybe forty-three? It didn't matter. There were more strawberries to eat.

"Stop that!" cried the now all-too-familiar voice of Mayor Sprinkle Shortbread III.

Blep smelled the sweet scent of her cake-like breath, even from across the clearing. But he continued to eat. He needed a steady distraction from the other delicious, delicious unicorns.

"We have you surrounded," said the mayor.

If Blep had been looking at her, he would have seen the furrow in her brow and her angry expression. It was one of the only times Mayor Shortbread had made such an angry face.

Blep instead continued to eat, doing his best to ignore the idea that strawberries went so well with shortbread.

"You're doing it again!" shouted the mayor.

Blep looked over to Ronk. The odd greenish zombie unicorn was smelling the mayor's sweet scent, too.

"We've caught you in the act this time!" the mayor continued.

And it wasn't just the mayor. There were other unicorns all around them. They smelled of marshmallows, of cookies, of brownie mixture. Blep tried to keep his mind on the strawberries.

"You've been stealing from us for months!"

By the time Blep smelled fudge and caramel behind him, it was already too late. He was worked up into a frenzy.

"This crime will not go unpunished!"

Blep's head jutted up out of the strawberry patch. He turned around in a fury. His eyes glowed a sickly yellow colour in the moonlight.

Beside him, Ronk turned as well. They were both staring at Mayor Shortbread and her many delicious fellow unicorns. There were so many flavours. Blep began to drool. Ronk had already been doing that very thing for the last few minutes.

"Why are you looking at me like that?" asked the mayor. She giggled. It sounded nervous this time.

Blep and Ronk shot off towards Mayor Shortbread. They were nearly across the clearing and about to pounce when a man fell to the ground between them and their prey.

"I confess!" the man shouted. "I confess to everything!"

The whole thing was weird enough to stop Blep and Ronk in their tracks. This slender man with grey hair was yelling at the top of his voice.

It had brought them back to their senses, if only for a moment.

"I've been stealing from Pegasia for months now! It was me!" yelled Gregory.

As if waiting for the most dramatic moment, Cradie, Xander and Bubblegum Taffy stepped out of the shadows.

"Meet your actual thief, Madame Mayor," Cradie said with a crooked smile.

"He used to run a toy shop," said Xander. "I wondered why he changed it to a sweet shop a few months ago."

Gregory stood up and dusted himself off. He seemed ready to confess. It was as if his guilt had been weighing on him for too long.

"Times have been hard," Gregory said. He looked at the ground as he spoke. "Ever since that portal mysteriously appeared in my storeroom,

I realized I could . . . I could get free stock if I just made regular trips here. I didn't think anyone would miss what I took. Not too much, at least."

"I rest my case!" said Bubblegum Taffy, perhaps a little too victoriously. Certainly the proclamation came a bit early.

"The only thing we're guilty of," said Cradie, "is wanting to come home. But we realize that's not a possibility any more."

Mayor Shortbread looked from Gregory to Cradie and then to Bubblegum Taffy. Then she smiled her perfect unicorn grin. "Thank goodness!" she said in her overly sweet way. "We have no idea how to run a legal system."

"You don't say," said Cradie jokingly.

"Why don't we all retire to the Town Hall and work this out," said the mayor, her voice practically bubbling with enthusiasm.

"You smell so nice," said Blep. While he had calmed down quite a bit, the faded red zombie unicorn had made his way over to the mayor.

"Or maybe we should just go," said Xander.

When Blep started sniffing her hair, the mayor quickly agreed.

# CHAPTER FOURTEEN

"RONK!"

"BLEP!"

"CRADIE!"

The Rainbow-Barfing Unicorns had been living up to their name more than usual ever since they returned to Earth. One rainbow after another had shot out of the Henderson Landfill all through the night and now into the morning. They had a lot of sweets to work out of their systems.

"Wow," said Xander. "You guys really need to get some solid food in you."

"Rotten food would be better," said Cradie as she burped.

"You OK?" said Xander. He picked up a tin of expired beetroot on the ground. It had been stacked on twenty or thirty other dented tins of equally expired beetroot. Xander wondered briefly why someone had thrown away so many tins, and then focused again on the issue at hand.

"I'm fine," said Cradie. "It was hard saying goodbye to Bubblegum again. I just thought we'd have more time."

"Yeah, the mayor seemed to want us out of there," said Xander.

"We barely had a chance to hug before they sent us on our way and sealed up the portal behind us," said Cradie.

"It could have been worse," said Xander. "You could have bitten her goodbye."

Cradie tried to laugh, but it came out more like a cough. For a second, Xander was worried that she might barf again.

"I understand why they had to close the portal," said Cradie.

"If you ask me, they let Gregory off too easy," said Blep. He was sitting on the dirt near Ronk, both munching on a pile of old trainers.

"I just . . . I just wish I'd had the chance to say the things I wanted to say," said Cradie. "So she knows how I feel about her."

Xander suddenly remembered where he was when he first saw Bubblegum Taffy. He remembered Kelly at the party, waiting for her lemonade. And he remembered all the things he was going to tell her but didn't.

Maybe today should be the day. Maybe Xander should leave the dump, march right over to Kelly's house and tell her everything. His shorts were dry by now. So he had that going for him.

Then Xander noticed Cradie walking over to a patch of dirt that was slightly hidden from the rest of the group by a broken and over-stuffed armchair.

"Cradie?" he said.

"I just want to be alone," Cradie said. But her voice didn't sound sad. It sounded just the opposite, in fact.

Xander took a few steps and peered around the stained chair. Cradie's eyes went wide as she looked up at him. In her teeth were a few strands of something that looked suspiciously like hair.

"Did you bite off some of Bubblegum's mane when you were hugging her goodbye?" Xander said, almost in a scolding voice.

"No," said Cradie as she gobbled up the evidence.

Xander smiled despite himself. He just had to wait. The rainbow that was sure to appear in the next few seconds would be all the proof that he needed.

# CHARACTER SPOTLIGHT:
# CRADIE!

Height: 1 metre 50 centimetres

Horn length: 17 centimetres

Weight (before barfing): 68 kilograms

Weight (after barfing): 57 kilograms

Colour: purplish

Barf colour: full spectrum

The totally unofficial leader of the
Rainbow-Barfing Unicorns – and the
lone female of the troublesome trio.
She's also the least disgusting zombie
of the bunch. Cradie has a sharp mind,
a sharp wit and a sharp horn.

# GLOSSARY

**banish** send someone away from a place and order them not to return

**bray** make a sound like the call of a donkey

**dimension** place in space and time

**dramatic** very noticeable

**expression** look on someone's face

**nefarious** very wicked

**portal** door or passage to another place

**spectrum** range of colours shown when light shines through water or a prism

# BARF WORDS

blow chunks barf

heave barf

hork barf

hurl barf

puke barf

ralph barf

regurgitate barf

retch barf

spew barf

throw up barf

upchuck barf

vomit barf

yak barf

# JOKES!!

What do Rainbow-Barfing Unicorns wear to work?

UNI-forms!

What is a Rainbow-Barfing Unicorn's favourite kind of rubbish scraps?

Unicorn on the cob.

What's a Rainbow-Barfing Unicorn's favourite mode of travel?

Unicycle!

Why don't Rainbow-Barfing Unicorns wear shoes?

They can't tie rain-bows!

How do Rainbow-Barfing Unicorns wash their hair?

In a bubble barf.

Why do Rainbow-Barfing unicorns always stick together?

They are a uni-fied group.

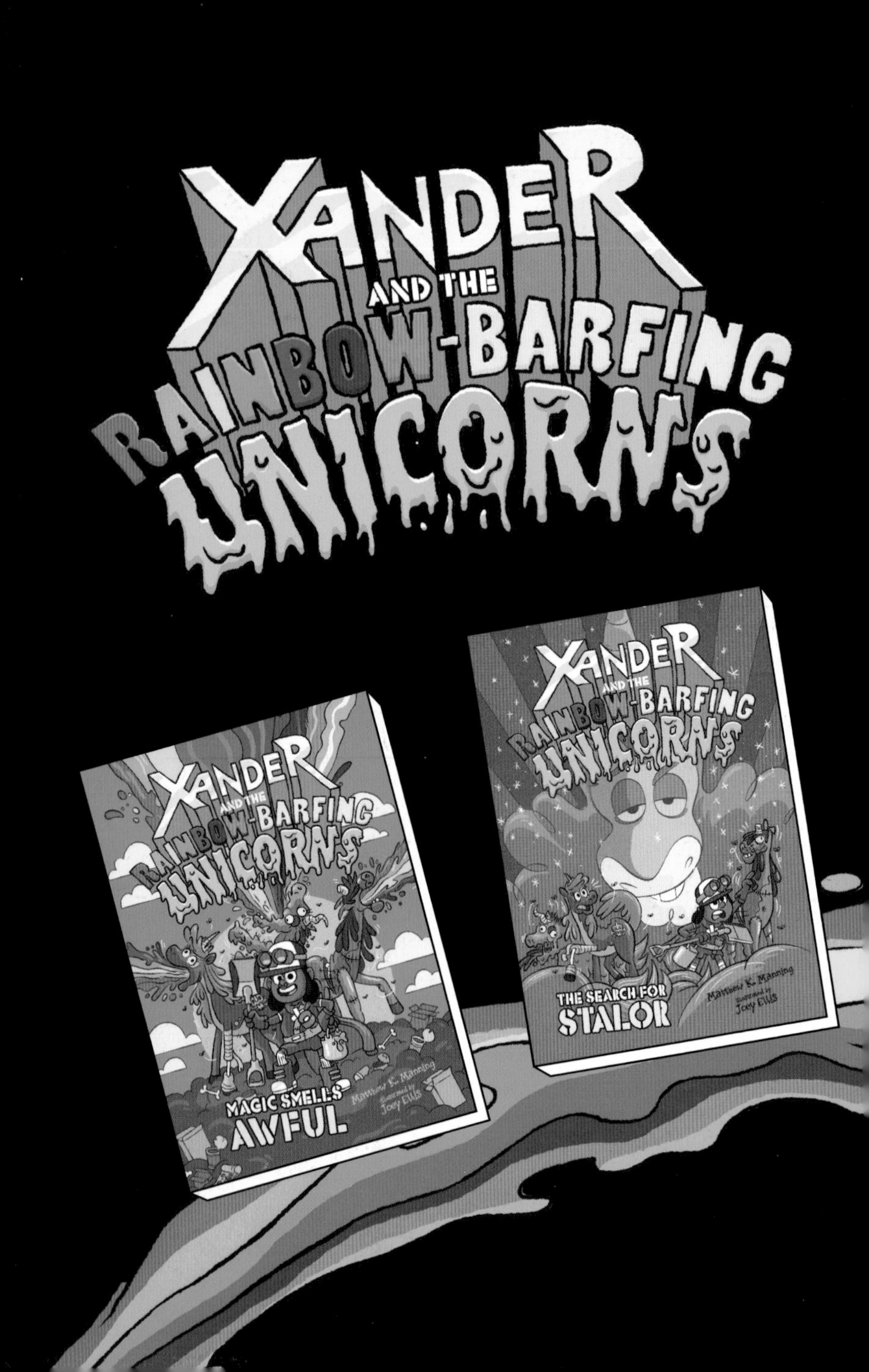
XANDER
AND THE
RAINBOW-BARFING
UNICORNS
XANDER
AND THE
RAINBOW-BARFING
UNICORNS
MAGIC SMELLS
AWFUL
Matthew K. Manning
Joey Ellis
XANDER
AND THE
RAINBOW-BARFING
UNICORNS
THE SEARCH FOR
STALOR
Matthew K. Manning
Joey Ellis

# READ THEM ALL!

# AUTHOR

The author of over seventy-five books, Matthew K. Manning has written several comic books as well, including the hit *Batman/ Teenage Mutant Ninja Turtles Adventures* miniseries. Currently the writer of the new IDW comic book series *Rise of the Teenage Mutant Ninja Turtles*, Manning has also written comics starring Batman, Wonder Woman, Spider-Man, the Justice League, the Looney Tunes and Scooby-Doo. He currently lives in North Carolina, USA, with his wife, Dorothy, and their two daughters, Lillian and Gwendolyn.

# ILLUSTRATOR

Joey Ellis lives and works in North Carolina, USA, with his wife, Erin, and two sons. Joey writes and draws for books, magazines, comics, games, big companies, small companies and everything else in between.